Sleep Pea Angel
and Doubtful Davie

The Sleep Pea Angel Adventure Series

DiAnn Y. Mason

AuthorHouse™
1663 Liberty Drive, Suite 200
Bloomington, IN 47403
www.authorhouse.com
Phone: 1-800-839-8640

AuthorHouse™ UK Ltd.
500 Avebury Boulevard
Central Milton Keynes, MK9 2BE
www.authorhouse.co.uk
Phone: 08001974150

First published by AuthorHouse 3/29/2007

ISBN: 978-1-4259-3390-6 (sc)

Library of Congress Control Number: 2006908134

Printed in the United States of America
Bloomington, Indiana

This book is printed on acid-free paper.

Bloomington, IN      Milton Keynes, UK

authorHOUSE®

Dedication

This first book in the Sleep Pea Angel series is dedicated to my first love: my dad - David A. Mason Sr.

Dad, you are my angel who watches over me day and night. Thank you for your love, support, guidance and friendship. I wish you were here to share this with me, but I feel in my heart that you've been with me every step of the way. I'll treasure every memory of you in my heart forever.

I love YOU!

DiAnn

Acknowledgments

Most importantly, I thank God for everything! "The greatest gift given to each of us daily is our life. The greatest gift we can give back is how we choose to spend each day of our life." – DiAnn Y. Mason

To my dear family and friends, I will always be thankful for the numerous ways each of you have loved, inspired and encouraged me throughout my life. My life shines brighter because of you!

I also thank some very special people who believed in Sleep Pea Angel from the beginning and shared my vision for this beautiful little angel. To Beverly Brown, Editor and LaJauna Guillory: You each gave the best of your time, talent and excitement to make Sleep Pea Angel a reality. Words can't adequately express my gratitude and appreciation for your support and dedication to both ventures: Sleep Pea Angel and Symphonic Expressions. To David Mason Jr. and Sue Youngblood: Thank you both for lending your assistance in your professional areas of expertise; I learned so much from you in the process.

To Juwana Jackson, Sheila Settles and Vikki Stone: Everything started with Symphonic Expressions and each of you believed in the possibilities and helped me brainstorm when SE was still in the womb. I will always be grateful for everything you were willing to share as SE became a reality. To Lulu Morris: Thank you for your encouragement, assistance and support with Symphonic Expressions and giving me your feedback on the first draft of the Sleep Pea Angel and Doubtful Davie story. To M.Kay duPont (www.yourwritingpartner.net): Thank you for taking the time to review this story while in the final phase. Your comments and suggestions were greatly appreciated and added the finishing touches. To Arthur Grier of A.L.G. Transportation Group: God spoke to me through you as you said those two words that would ignite my vision of Sleep Pea Angel. Thank you for the limo ride that changed my life!

Stay tuned everyone. There is so much more in store for our sweet little Sleep Pea Angel!

Love your friend … the dreamer

DiAnn

Do you know about the beautiful blue angel named Sleep Pea who was given a special pea from the ocean called Peadie that holds the names of all the children in the world?

You don't? Are you sure?

Well, you see, every night all the names of little boys and girls who can't get to sleep swirl around and around inside the special pea. Then all of a sudden only one name appears. No one ever knows just what name it will be.

Sleep Pea Angel visits that little boy or girl and helps them get to sleep. Maybe one night when you can't sleep, she'll come to visit you too. Gee, I wonder who she'll visit tonight.

And so our story begins ...

Sleep Pea Angel rubbed her eyes, yawned and stretched her arms as wide as she could stretch them.

She looked around and said, "Wake up, wake up, my precious little Peadie. It's time to find out who needs our help tonight."

Sleep Pea Angel smiled to herself and began to sing:

"I'm as lucky as can be, as I was given this special pea that holds the names of boys and girls who need my help through out the world.

"Every night as I look into my precious little Peadie, a special child's name appears to me. This child is having trouble sleeping at night because something is going on that's not quite right."

As Sleep Pea Angel looked closer, she saw nine letters: A-I-K-N-D-E-I-G-V. Now what could A I K N D E I G V spell? Once again the letters began swirling around and around until they spelled the name DAVIE KING!

"Poor Davie King," Sleep Pea Angel said. "I wonder why he is having trouble sleeping tonight." So she gently rubbed her pea, and this is what she saw …

There were three children at the black board working on math problems. It was now Davie's turn. His teacher asked him if he knew the answer to his math problem: 6 + 3 = ?

Davie spoke in his very low tone, "I doubt it."

"You doubt it?" his teacher asked. "OK, Davie, can you answer the next math problem: 5 + 3 = ?"

Davie just hung his head and said, "I doubt it."

All the children in the class started laughing, saying, "Poor little Davie King; he doubts just about everything."

"Class, class, please be quiet. Davie, if you are not going to do your school work, I'm going to take you to the principal's office. Now, I'm going to ask you one more time. Are you going to do your school work?"

Davie just shrugged his shoulders, and said, "I doubt it."

"OK, young man, off to the principal's office you go. She turned to the class saying, "All of you stay in your seats and continue working on your math problems. Davie, let's go." Then she marched Davie down to the principal's office. His teacher said, "Davie, sit right here while I go in to talk to the principal."

The principal called his mom, Mrs. King, who came to school right away. They told her what Davie had done today.

Mrs. King said, "I'm sorry Davie didn't do his school work. He really is a good boy. His father and I will talk to him."

Davie just rested his head in his hands and sighed, because he knew what was in store for him when he got home.

You see, this wasn't the first time Davie had been sent home for disrupting the class.

"Davie, haven't your mom and I told you that you have to do your school work?" his dad asked.

Davie put his hands in his pockets and said, "I doubt it?"

"You doubt it," his dad said in an angry voice. Well, Mr. Smarty Pants, you can just go to your room and go to bed!"

A little later, his mom poked her head through Davie's bedroom door and said, "Davie, do you want to talk?"

Davie just shook his head and said, "I doubt it" while turning over in his bed.

So his mom closed the door and went back downstairs. Davie thought to himself, "See, no one even cares!" He began to cry and could not fall asleep. He thought, "I'm really not that bad."

Or was he?

Sleep Pea Angel had seen enough and tucked Peadie in her pouch, thinking to herself, "I must go at once. Little Davie really needs me." So she said a silent prayer, got up from her cloud and took to the air.

She flew over oceans, rivers and streams. Over mountains, deserts, grass and trees. As Sleep Pea Angel passed each star, she always said hello, for they guided her way no matter how far.

Sleep Pea Angel asked one of the stars, "Am I there yet?"

"Not yet, Sleep Pea Angel, but very soon I bet." Each star became brighter as she passed by, but the very last star was the brightest in the sky. It was shining ever so brightly to let Sleep Pea Angel know that this is the home of the child, Davie King, who can't sleep.

Sleep Pea Angel looked into the bedroom window and saw Davie lying awake in his bed. She tapped on the window and quietly said, "Hi, Davie, it's me, Sleep Pea Angel. May I come in?"

Davie closed his eyes real tight and counted to three. When he opened his eyes, he was surprised to see that she had not gone away. Again she tapped on the window saying, "Hi, Davie, it's me, Sleep Pea Angel. May I come in?"

Davie said with a frown, "I guess so, but why are you here? What do you want with me?"

Sleep Pea Angel opened the window and flew into Davie's room. As she came closer, she saw such a sad little boy.

Davie sat straight up in his bed and said, "How can this be true? Sleep Pea Angel, or whatever your name is, I don't even believe in you!"

Sleep Pea Angel smiled and said, "I came because you needed to know that someone cares and to help you find a better way to answer a question. Saying 'I doubt it' all the time gets you into trouble with your teacher, mom and dad."

Davie said with a frown, "I doubt that you can do anything to help me."

Sleep Pea Angel said, "Davie, I think I see what's bothering you, but let me just ask you a question or two. Do you now believe that I am real?"

Davie said, "Yes, I guess the stories I heard from those silly kids at school are true. Sleep Pea Angel does exist. There really is a you!"

"Why do you call the kids at school silly?" asked Sleep Pea Angel.

Davie thought for a minute and said, "Because they laugh at me and tease me, saying, poor little Davie King; he doubts just about everything!"

"Yes, Davie, it isn't very nice for the kids at school to laugh and make fun of you, but you do know that your mom and dad really care, don't you?" Sleep Pea Angel asked.

Davie folded his arms and said, "Sometimes I just doubt Mom and Dad really care about me. They get mad at me and make me go straight to bed without playing video games or watching TV."

Sleep Pea Angel said, "Davie, just because your mom and dad send you to bed without TV doesn't mean they don't care about you. I know that they love you very, very much."

Sleep Pea Angel waved her hand over Davie and said, "I want you to close your eyes real tight. I have a few special things to show you tonight. Now open your eyes when I count to three ... One, Two, Three!"

Davie opened his eyes and saw himself as a little baby in his crib. His mom and dad were standing over him saying, "We are so happy to have this beautiful baby boy."

Davie was still frowning, so Sleep Pea Angel waved her hand again and a new scene appeared.

The next thing Davie saw was his mom and dad tucking him safe and sound into his bed saying, "Davie, we're so glad you had a good time at your birthday party and that you loved your present. We know how much you really wanted that new red bike. We love you so very much!"

Davie was silent for a moment. Then his frown turned upside down, and he was smiling from ear to ear. He said to himself, "I remember that birthday party. It was so much fun, and I was so happy to get my new red bike!"

Davie began jumping up and down on his bed saying, "I guess Mom and Dad really love me very much. Now I see just what a lucky boy I am. When I go to school tomorrow, I'm going to tell my teacher that I'm sorry for the way I acted in school today. I can add my numbers!" Davie used his fingers and said, "3 + 7 = 10 and 4 + 5 = 9!

"Thank you, Sleep Pea Angel, for coming to see me tonight. Now I know that everything is going to be all right!"

Sleep Pea Angel kissed Davie good night and tucked him back in bed real tight. "Sweet dreams, little Davie King. Always do your best in school. Tomorrow, be sure to tell the kids all about our visit. Good night."

Sleep Pea Angel was so happy that her wings began to flap, her hands began to clap, and she began to dance around singing:

"I want all the children in the world to know just how much I love them so! Every night my precious Peadie tells me the name of the special child I need to see!"

Then she flew out of the window and followed the stars home. She thought to herself, "What a wonderful visit I had with Davie. He just needed to know how much he was loved. I can't wait to see whom I will visit next."

Yes, Sleep Pea Angel felt good about her visit with Davie and was sure that, from now on, Davie King was going to be just fine.

She said to her little pea as she fluffed her cloud until it was just right, "Time to go to sleep, my precious little Peadie, for tomorrow we have someone new to see. Good night."

Sleep Pea Angel wants to know ...

What do **YOU** think?

1) Why was Davie doubtful?

2) Are you a 'Doubtful Davie' sometimes?

   If you are, why?

3) Why was Davie sent to bed without being able to watch TV or play video games?

4) Do you ever find it hard to do your school work?

   If you do, why?

5) What are some things you can do to help someone who is doubtful?

Sleep Pea Angel's A B C's

<u>A</u>lways <u>B</u>elieve YOU <u>C</u>an!!

Sleep Pea Angel would love to hear from you ...
Send her an email at spa@sleeppeaangel.com

Look for the second book in the Sleep Pea Angel series. Who will be the next special child that Sleep Pea Angel will visit? Who knows ... maybe it will be YOU!

About the Author

DiAnn Y. Mason is an exciting new author and poet who is taking the literary scene by storm. She has written and journaled for personal enjoyment throughout every stage of her life. However, it wasn't until her children were grown that she discovered her true calling and passion for writing. DiAnn creates beautifully framed one-of-a-kind personalized poetry for that special person, event or occasion in your life (www.symphonicexpressions.com). In addition, she has written hundreds of poems for every aspect of life, including her own special collection of children's nursery rhymes.

She has two children, Amber and Gary, who are a true inspiration to her. She is a cancer survivor with a zest and zeal for all that life has to offer. One of her favorite sayings is, "If not now, when?" Currently she is working on the second and third books in the new children's series, Sleep Pea Angel. She is also working on her first novel which is set for release in 2007.

DiAnn is an excellent speaker and entertains any age audience with life experiences, while providing a realistic view on the importance of making each day stand on its own. She enjoys the opportunity to read her stories to children. If you are interested in having DiAnn as a guest speaker or write an article for your publication, please contact her at info@symphonicexpressions.com

"Live your life to the fullest: it's the greatest gift you'll ever receive." - DiAnn Y. Mason

About the Sleep Pea Angel Adventure Series

The Sleep Pea Angel Adventure Series by DiAnn Y. Mason is a delightful and heart-warming collection of special stories that teach children valuable life lessons. Each one is painstakingly illustrated with colorful characters and scenery. They are the perfect story time or bedtime books for young children.

The main character is Sleep Pea Angel. She is a beautiful blue angel who has a special pea she calls Peadie that contains the names of all the children throughout the world. Each night, the name of one child who is having trouble sleeping appears inside the pea. Sleep Pea Angel visits this special child and helps to resolve any issues that keep him or her from sleeping.

The first book in the series is about a little boy named Davie King, who doubts just about everything! Read the "Sleep Pea Angel and Doubtful Davie" story to find out how Sleep Pea Angel will help Davie get to sleep tonight.

Printed in the United States
78867LV00002B